Praise for
Madison Weatherbee
The Different Dachshund

"Barbara Kirshner's book takes the reader on a magical journey in the company of Madison, a sweet, endearing little dachshund in her search for love and happiness in a tough world. Reading this book made me think what it might've been like if Toto had travelled through Oz entirely on his own. Like Dorothy, like Madison, they're all out there on the road of life, walking, running, hiding, only to discover that, in the end, there's no place like home."

Jeff Bennett, Artistic Director of Bare Bones Theatre Company

Barbara Kirshner has written an inspirational, heart-warming story full of pathos, adventure and love. Madison is such a sweet, spunky doxie! The reader is on her side all the way through the book.

Anne Kelly-Edmunds, Creative writing instructor and author of The Promise, a book of poems

Madison Weatherbee is a heartwarming journey about finding love and acceptance in a sometimes scary world. Full of twists and turns, our heroine pup discovers friends and foes during her quest for a forever home. I laughed, I cried, I bit my nails. I fell in love with Madison!

Through this sweet, innocent pup, Barbara Kirshner celebrates the differences that make each and every one of us so special and unique.

JoAnn Havrilla, Actress of stage, screen and television

Madison Weatherbee

The Different Dachshund

By
Barbara Anne Kirshner

© October 2013

With special thanks to Gregg Jacoby for his constant
encouragement and support.

This is a work of fiction. While the protagonist, Madison,
was a real dachshund, the characters, places and incidents
are the product of the author's imagination or are used
fictitiously. Any resemblance to actual persons, living or
dead, events, or locales is entirely coincidental.

Published in the United States by CreateSpace.com,
a subsidiary of Amazon.com.

Library of Congress Cataloging-in-Publication Data

Kirshner, Barbara Anne

Madison Weatherbee-The Different Dachshund/Barbara
Anne Kirshner; photographs by Barbara Anne Kirshner;
graphic designs by Kim Mc Kenna- 1st edition

ISBN 978-0615995397

ISBN: 061599539X

LCCN: 2014906292

Barbara Anne Kirshner, Miller Place, NY

Printed in the United States of America

First Edition 2014

DEDICATION
*This book is lovingly dedicated
to
Madison Weatherbee Jacoby Kirshner
who inspired me daily
and taught me the meaning of
everlasting love and devotion.
Your valiant character,
even in the face of adversity,
combined with your unique presence
will live in my heart
forever.

IT ALL STARTED HERE

I WAS BORN someplace out in the Midwest. Missouri is what I overheard them say.

I really don't remember too much about that time. I can recall a warm, sweet scent licking at me and lots of brothers and sisters playing together. We used to climb over each other trying to get the attention of Momma, but she was so busy with all of us that I really didn't get too much. Everyone was bigger than I was, pushier, too. I didn't like nosing my way in, so I stayed hungry sometimes. But when I did get my turn, I always felt strong when I had Momma's milk. Things were pretty good.

There was a kind, gray-haired lady whom everyone called Granny Muriel. She would feed any of us with a tiny bottle if we didn't get enough to drink.

Granny Muriel had two grandkids, Katie and Tommy, who came over to play. They would cuddle me and I loved getting their attention. But then they would say something about the way I looked, something about a *scruff* at the back of my neck that stood out, making me different from the rest. I didn't know what a scruff was because I never saw the back of my neck.

I tried to.

I tried to whip my head around real fast, but that just made me dizzy.

I tried stretching as far as I could, but all I saw was my long body and my tail.

I looked at the back of my brothers' and sisters' necks, but I didn't see anything unusual about them. They all had soft red fur that rested smoothly. I figured I must look the same way, but I always wondered if I really was different.

One day Granny Muriel ran a finger down the back of my neck as she pondered, "I don't know if anyone will want you."

"She's the gentlest and friendliest pup," Katie pointed out.

Granny Muriel sighed and continued, "That she is, but most people come here looking for perfect dachshunds. I don't know if they will see beyond the scruff."

My days were pretty happy with Momma watching over us while we chased and pawed at each other.

But then one day I overheard Granny Muriel tell her grandkids, "Well it looks like tomorrow I'm getting people coming by to purchase some of these here pups. So say your good-byes and wish them well in their new homes. You won't be seeing the whole litter the next time you visit."

3

"Awww, no!" exclaimed both grandkids.

Katie confided to Tommy, "It's such fun when the pups are born and then we get to play with them. But when they have to go, it's always sad. At least one of these pups won't be here when we visit tomorrow and the rest will be gone soon, too."

She looked at all of us and then added, "Well, we can be almost sure who will be left behind. I don't think the people will take that scruffy pup, not when all the others are so beautiful and perfect."

When they left the room, I trotted over to a floor-length mirror and tried again to stretch my head around so I could see that scruff-thing they were all talking about.

Will anyone ever want me?

What will happen to me if no one wants me?

Sure enough, the people came as planned. They looked us over and made selections. A lady pointed to me and admitted to Granny, "This one has such a pretty face and I would have picked her if it hadn't been for that scruff thing."

Soon my brothers and sisters were all gone. I missed them, but now I had Momma all to myself. I loved having all of her attention and I even got first choice of the toys and bones Granny Muriel gave us.

Today I got to chew on one of my favorite bones...*Mmmmm*...it tasted mighty good against my brand new set of baby teeth. I tried to keep the chomping down so I wouldn't wake Momma from her mid-afternoon nap.

Y-*A*-*W*-*N*!

Hmm, maybe I could use a little snooze too. I put my bone aside, stretched my hind legs, then my front and plopped down curling up with my back against Momma's warm, soft tummy.

In the distance, I heard the squeak of the old rickety front door. The voices of

Granny Muriel and Uncle Henry grew louder as they made their way into the den where we were resting. My ears perked up to catch the end of what Granny Muriel muttered. It was about someone going away and Uncle Henry told her that the pickup truck was ready.

"It's just too bad we couldn't find a nice home for the pup right here in town. I do so like to see our pups grow with the families that get them," Granny Muriel lamented.

Uncle Henry chuckled and remarked, "Aw, you're just an old softie. Well, I'll go out to the truck and you get our little girl ready for her trip." Uncle Henry's heavy footsteps grew quieter as he made his way to the front of the house letting the screen door shut behind him.

The stillness lulled me into a twilight sleep that was quickly jarred when Granny Muriel scooped me up from my comfort place beside Momma. In a half-daze, I could hardly believe what looked like a dark cave coming toward me. Granny Muriel swung open a door made of metal bars, stuffed me inside, then shut and bolted the door. I whimpered and paced furiously back and forth. Momma woke from her nap and gazed almost dreamily over her shoulder in my direction. Her puzzled expression turned into a deep frown when she realized what was happening. She raced over to me and touched the bars with her paw. I licked at Momma's fingers through the slats begging her to get me out of here.

"I'm sorry, old girl, but it's time for this pup to go," Granny Muriel said.

Momma howled as she scratched at the metal bars.

"Oh, you're breaking my heart, old girl." Granny Muriel thought for a minute then gave in. "OK, one last good-bye," she added.

Granny Muriel slid back the bolt and the gate popped open. I ran over to Momma, licked her many times on her eyes, then tried to get a last sniff of her warm, sweet milky scent. She nuzzled me, spreading wet kisses over my forehead and the back of my neck where they say I have that *scruff* thing. Then Granny Muriel caught me up again and tossed me back into that cold, frightful case. The gate clamped shut and the bolt slid into place. "I'm sorry to do this to you, little one, but I just can't keep you even though you're a very good girl, just like your momma."

I stood quivering.

What did I do that was so bad?

Why did I get locked up in this terrible place?

Why couldn't I stay here with Momma?

The quiver that spread through my whole body wouldn't stop. I swayed from side to side, losing my balance as Granny Muriel carried me out of the farmhouse. The whining that came from deep down in my throat made it hard for me to swallow.

Where were they sending me?

Will I ever see Momma again?

9

Will I ever get out of this cold, dark place?

Uncle Henry waited by the pickup truck like he promised. Granny Muriel slipped my carry case onto the back bed of the truck and slammed the panel shut.

"See you later," Uncle Henry called out.

Off we went…

… *away* from Momma,

… *away* from Granny Muriel and the grandkids,

… *away* from the farm, the only home I've ever known.

I pushed my nose through the opening between the bars of the carry case. Momma was at the front door.

As we pulled away, I could still hear Momma's frantic howling.

I TAKE TO THE SKIES

THE TRUCK MADE a loud r-u-m-m-m-m-m noise as it rumbled down the dirt driveway, tossing me from side to side.

I was in a dark, cold case, going away from Momma, Granny Muriel and the grand-kids, away from everything that was familiar to me. The pick-up truck bounced over a hill, popping me so far up that I hit my head then flopped to the floor and that's when all the moving stopped.

The back panel of the truck creaked open. Uncle Henry lifted the case and car-ried me into a noisy building. I stuck my nose between the bars and sniffed. The air was dull and stuffy, no longer filled with the yummy smells of sweet peas and strawberries growing on Granny Muriel's farm. I pressed my head against the bars trying to see out. There were lots of people scurrying around with carry bags-large ones, smaller ones, some on rollers, and some with shoulder straps.

Uncle Henry put my case down. His voice sounded kind as he spoke to a woman dressed in blue standing behind a counter. "Take good care of this here pup," he explained. "She's going off to New York to find herself a home."

"Don't worry, she'll be fine," the woman assured him.

And with that I was transferred to something that was moving. I was handed off from one person to another and another until I wound up inside a place so dark I had to squint to see what was around me. I was surrounded by piles of big bags like the ones people were rolling and holding.

I tried to lie down, but felt so restless. I rolled onto my back and stared up at the ceiling of the carry case. My tummy grumbled; I was starving. That's when I smelled it, a faint hint of something sweet. I stood up, sniffed between the bars of the case trying to search out the direction of the scent. I grew hungrier with the sugary aroma filling my nose, but here I was stuck in this case. There had to be a way out.

The door made of metal bars was fastened by one single cross bar going through a loop attached to the cage. If I could jiggle that bolt, maybe it would give way and set me free. I pressed my nose against the end of it and pushed sideways.

Ouch!

It pinched me!

I hit the end of the rod with my paw… once…twice. It didn't even budge. I opened my toes real wide so I could get the pad of my paw on it and I swung with all my might. The

14

bar scraped against the loop as it moved back a bit. It was so close to opening now. One more swat would surely set me free. Gearing up, I punched the metal strip. It squeaked and the barrier slid back popping the door wide open!

I was FREE!

Now the only thing that kept me away from the sweet smell was all these rows of piled bags. But that wasn't going to stop me. I crawled over some large ones, wiggled between others and pushed my way through. I squeezed between heavy suitcases that wouldn't budge and softer bags that gave way ever so slightly. My long body squirmed around extended handles and wheels. The sugary aroma filled my nostrils. The food was almost within reach. All that stood between me and my supper was a very tall, rectangular case. I stretched out my front legs and took a flying leap. My body plunged head first over that tall case. I smacked into a large, scratchy sack that toppled over and sent long horn-shaped leafy things rolling in all directions.

15

What luck! I knew the treasure that lay inside the leaves or husks as Uncle Henry called them. Momma and I often made our way through Uncle Henry's corn fields, searching for an ear with a loose husk that was easy to tear away. I nosed through my find until I happened upon one that was sure to open. I pulled a leaf with my teeth and yanked it back revealing the luscious yellow treasure within.

As I tore into the corn gobbling at the crunchy sweetness, I heard a whimper and something moving. Maybe I wasn't alone.

Grasping the corn in my mouth, I headed in the direction of the sound. I came upon a pile of bags that formed a tunnel and squeezed between them. There on the other side was a carry case similar to mine. I approached it and looked inside. Sure enough, there was a pup. It was small like me, but it had lots of white curls. And it was a girl, just like me. She poked her nose between the bars of her case and sniffed at me. I set my corn aside and we sniffed a lot at each other to ensure that we had not met up with an enemy.

The pup was wearing a red coat. It looked so pretty over the white curls. I wish I had a coat like that. I would feel a lot warmer if I had one. The curly pup started to wag her tail so I knew she was friendly. I wagged back to let her know I wanted to be friends.

A tear dropped from the curly pup's eye and she whimpered, "It's so scary in here and I'm so hungry. I'm glad I'm not alone. Do you think you could open this case so I could get something to eat?"

17

"I'll try," I promised and examined her carry case.

Hers had a cross bar just like mine, but there was something else hanging from it. I didn't know what it was. I opened my toes wide like I did to get my case to open and I hit the bar, but it didn't move. That wasn't going to stop me. I backed up then hurled my entire body at it. The force sent me flying backward and I smacked into surrounding bags. I sat up and shook off the pain. That thing sticking out seemed to be keeping the rod from sliding open.

I looked helplessly at the curly pup and admitted, "I don't think I can get you out."

"Thanks anyway for trying, but I'm still so hungry."

I picked up a piece of the corn with my mouth, brought it over to her carry case and tried to push it through the bars. The curly pup wagged her tail. The corn wouldn't go through, but the pup tore away at what she could get. She pulled out chunks and swallowed them up. I held the ear of corn with all my might until my mouth ached so much that I dropped it.

"Thank you. I'm feeling much better now. I don't know why my lady didn't leave me a snack, but thanks for helping."

"You're very welcome," I replied.

Just then I heard a loud *thump* followed by a clanging and shifting like something was opening.

MY ROMP THROUGH JFK AIRPORT AND MY FIRST SHUTTLE RIDE

A BIG DOOR opened sending streams of light into the cabin. Heavy footsteps grew closer forcing me to search out a hiding place. I pushed my way between some bags creating a tunnel near the wall. Luggage was being shuffled around. I peeked out and saw a tall man move farther in as he tossed bags toward the light. I held my breath and remained perfectly still, not wanting him to see me.

His voice was loud as he called to someone behind him, "There's supposed to be two pups on this trip. Oh, yeah, there's one right here." He picked up the curly pup's carry case and handed her over to another man waiting just outside the door. Then he came back inside and said, "Now, for the other pup..."

He looked around until he found my carry case. "Oh, here it is." He picked up the case and gasped, "Wait a minute! The latch is open. There's no pup in here! The pup got away!"

"Where could it go? Just look," the voice from outside implored.

"I'm looking, but I don't see anything. Here's the carry case." He handed out my case.

I slinked my way through the tunnel made by the stacked luggage and padded lightly toward the open door. As the man handed out my carry case, I scurried around his legs and fled. The glaring sunlight blinded me, but I shot downstairs, dodged the other man and sprinted across a big field. My ears flapped as I raced away.

"Look! There it is! There's the pup!" the other man shouted.

"Go and get that little runt!" the man at the door commanded. "We'll be in big trouble if it gets lost!"

Footsteps pounded at a distance behind me. I ducked into a building and jumped up onto a moving belt that held lots of suitcases. But the ones in front of me disappeared through a dark opening that soon took me, shooting me down a large tube and spitting me onto a moving thing surrounded by people.

"Look Dad, a dog!" a young boy exclaimed.

People turned, looked at me and yelled, "A dog!"

I leaped off the moving thing, scrambled between bags and hid behind a garbage can. The people were excited now.

"Did you see that pup?"

"The pup, where did it go?"

"It was just here."

"Someone better get it."

"How could a pup get loose in an airport?"

Mixed in with all the exclamations was a soft lady's voice cooing, "I'm so glad you're OK, my beautiful Missy."

Craning my neck out from behind the garbage can, I saw a lady lifting the curly pup out of her carry case. The lady gave her a great big hug.

Why couldn't someone give me a great big hug like that?

The curly pup glanced in my direction as the lady cradled her. She gave the woman several licks on her cheek, looked towards me again, then turned away to lick the woman's lips. The lady giggled with joy and kissed the curly pup on her forehead.

It was as if that pup was showing off to me. She had someone to love her, feed her and give her kisses. I had nothing-no home, no food, and no one to love me. Where could I go? Granny Muriel sent me away, so I couldn't go back home to Momma.

Watching the curly pup look so cozy in the arms of that lady, I knew what would make me happy again. I had to find a new home with a family who would love me and hug me like that lady hugged the curly pup. Yes, that's what I wanted most of all!

My daydream was suddenly interrupted by the voices of the two men from the plane. "Anyone see a loose pup here?" they shouted.

"Yes, we did see a pup, but we don't know where it went," several people reported.

I needed to get out of here. At a distance I saw glass doors open and close as people went through them. That was my way out, but there was a big open space between the garbage can and those doors. My body trembled as I came out from behind the can and raced across the floor.

That's when I heard one of the men yell, "There! There's the pup! Someone grab it!"

My body quaked with fear, but I took a deep breath and sprinted. I scrambled around feet and rushed out those doors toward a busy street. Cars sped by inches from where I stood.

"Where's that pup? It'll get lost out here," voices said from behind me.

There was a nearby staircase, my only way out. I bounded up those stairs just as a long, rattling thing was coming.

I heard someone say, "Good, the shuttle is right on time."

I didn't know what a shuttle was, but I figured I'd find out. The doors opened and I scooted onboard and hid under one of the seats. Lots of feet shuffled past me. Soon the doors closed and the shuttle took off. It moved so fast I could hardly keep myself from falling over. It's a good thing I have short legs and I'm really close to the ground.

After a little while, the shuttle shrieked and jerked sending me rolling under other seats. The doors whipped open and all the people rushed out. I followed them.

I saw a lady carrying a great big shopping bag that was even bigger than I was. I stayed real close to her bag so no one would see me. We were on a wide deck when another shuttle roared up and screeched to a stop. I followed the lady with the shopping bag on to this other shuttle. Doors slammed shut and we were off again.

I ducked under a seat. We went into a dark place and the shuttle suddenly quivered, then seemed to sigh as it came to a stop. The lady was on her feet again and she edged toward the door. I knew I had to make a run for it, so I dashed around her feet and the feet of other passengers.

From behind me there were shouts of, "Look over there! There's a pup!"

"Someone should get it!"

"Are there dog tags? That pup must be lost."

I thought to myself, what are dog tags? I hurried down a long platform and weaved between legs. Behind me I heard anxious voices.

"What's that?"

"Oh, look! A dog!"

"Catch it before it heads into traffic!"

What were they talking about? Traffic? What's traffic?

Madison Weatherbee- The Different Dachshund

I MEET NEW YORK CITY

I GOT TO the top of the stairs and I saw what traffic was. There were yellow cars honking and speeding by. I looked up as far as my neck would stretch and saw very tall buildings with walls of glass and stone. One thing was for sure, I wasn't anywhere near Granny Muriel's farm.

There were lots of people rushing past me. They didn't look like the people back home either, because they wore suits and dresses. Granny Muriel saved her best dress only for Sunday when she went to church.

Somehow I didn't think these people were going off to church.

"Psst."

I looked around, but saw no one at my level. I heard it again, a little louder than before, "PSST!" That's when I saw it across the busy street. A small, gray mouse waved its paw bidding me to cross over to it. What luck, a mouse! I'm not sure why it called me. After all, I'm a dachshund. Didn't it know I hunt mice? That mouse stood on his hind legs and leaned against a tall pole with a light on top of it. He called to me in a high-pitched, squeaky voice, "Hey! Over here! I bet you can't catch me!"

That's all I needed to hear. Why, I'll show him! Off I shot into that busy street, dodging those yellow cars. A screech of tires caught me off guard and I froze right there in the middle of the street. A man leaned his head out the window of one of those big yellow cars and yelled, "Hey, get out of the road!" The car was so close that it almost hit me.

A-h-h-h-h!

And that's when I heard it, a cackle, coming from that mouse. He stood on the sidewalk holding his belly as he laughed at me. That's it. I'll show him. I shook the fear off and raced in his direction. He escaped down a dark flight of stairs with me chasing after him. That mouse tried to get me killed and now he was going to pay!

At the bottom of the stairs was a platform and on either side were things similar to the tracks that came with Tommy's train set. Where was that no-good mouse?

Through the darkness I heard, "Hey, pup, what you waiting for? Maybe I should throw you a bone?"

That nasty mouse stood in the shadows at the end of the platform. I shot after him, but he scurried onto one of the tracks.

I chased him and ran deeper and deeper into darkness.

Then I heard it...a metal sound, like the rattling of the shuttle that took me to this place. I looked up and saw a big round light. What was that?!! It wasn't slowing down. It was coming at me!

I need to save myself! Jump!!

I jumped off the tracks just as the light reached me. Clinging to the wall, I tried to get back as far as I could. That train roared past, blowing wind and soot into my face. I gulped, closed my eyes and stood firm, waiting for that monster train to pass. As soon as it was gone, I gave out a great big *A-A-A-H-H-H!*

That's when I heard it again-that squeaky mouse voice teasing, "Hey, pup, you want me?"

I squinted to try to make out the mouse figure in the dark tunnel. Sure enough, there he was. That was it! That mouse almost got me killed twice! I lunged after him and we raced down the tunnel. All of a sudden, he stopped short. Why did he do that? I ran up to him and was about to put my paw out when a great big rat came out of the shadows and stood between us.

The rat snarled, "Hey, pup, you picking on my pal, Marvin?" With a slight turn of his head, he shouted over his shoulder, "Gang, lookie here at this pup bothering our boy, Marvin."

Out from the shadows came two more rats.

One grumbled, "We don't take too kindly to our buddy being pushed around."

The other sneered, "So, pup, what you want to do now? It's four against one."

They chanted, "Four against *one*...four against *one*...four against *one*."

The rats moved in on me. I had to escape the tunnel before the next train trapped me here. I had to get away from this nasty gang!

I backed up, turned and *raaaaaaaaaan* as fast as I could. I heard them cackling behind me, but I just kept running. I hopped onto the platform, sprang up the stairs until I made it to the busy streets.

WOW! That was a close call!

I stood there panting. *HUH! HUH! HUH!*

When I finally caught my breath, I started walking. I wandered aimlessly past tall buildings and all those yellow fast-moving cars. I came to a crossroads, looked up and saw lots of bright lights and pictures of very pretty people. The person standing next to me looked up too and, in an accent that was very different from Granny Muriel's, she announced, "This is Times Square."

"Isn't it colorful! Just look at all those neon lights," her companion exclaimed.

MY BROADWAY DEBUT

SO, THAT'S WHERE I was, a place called Times Square. Down one of the streets were lines of people waiting as if to get inside big glass doors. On either side of these doors were very large pictures of smiling people dressed in frilly clothes kicking their legs in the air. They looked like they were having so much fun that I wanted to join them.

I walked past all the people and saw a black door with these letters on it:

S-T-A-G-E-D-O-O-R

A screech of tires caught my attention. One of those yellow fast-moving cars pulled up and a real pretty lady got out. She walked over to that black door with the writing on it, turned the knob and was about to go inside when someone called, "Bev, hold the door!" Another woman rushed over.

The pretty lady turned to the other one giving me the chance to sneak inside before they could see me. A winding staircase loomed up in front of me, so I sneaked all the way to the top of the stairs. Lots of people were rushing around up there. They were all dressed in big, glittery clothes just like in the pictures outside and they called out to each other. Then I saw a man who was dressed in a white shirt and black pants. He shouted out the time to the glittery people.

They all looked like they were getting ready for something special. One group of people was in a big area stretching, kind of like I do when I first get up in the morning. Other people walked around humming. Some people made strange hooting noises. I don't know why they did that.

I tiptoed down the hall making sure to keep in the shadows so no one could see me. That man who was calling out the time bellowed, "Five minutes to curtain! Five minutes to curtain!" I didn't know what that meant, but suddenly all the stretching and humming and strange noises stopped. They gazed into mirrors and fixed their hair and makeup. Some ladies put on lipstick; anyway, that's what Granny Muriel used to call it when she painted her lips.

Now the time man boomed, "One minute to curtain! One minute to curtain!"

I heard some glittery people say to each other, "Break a leg!"

Other glittery people answered, "Yes, break legs!"

Why would they want to break legs? That would hurt and it wouldn't be very much fun.

As I inched my way down the dark hall glancing over my shoulder to make sure I wasn't seen, I tripped into something that splashed at me. To my surprise a saucer of milk was just sitting there. What luck! I was *so-o-o-o* thirsty! I slurped at the bowl thinking all the while that I couldn't remember the last time I had something to drink. This milk was sweet and cool.

YUM! Just what I needed! *YUM! YUM!*

"H-S-S-S-T…H-S-S-S-T"   *the milk belongs to a cat*

I jerked my head up from the saucer, my eyes darted wildly in the darkness. Who was that?

"You!"

"Who?"

"I'm talking to you."

39

"Me? Someone is talking to me?"

I spun my head around every which way trying to see the specter through the darkness.

"P-u-u-u-u-r-r-r"

Was it talking to me?

"Where are your manners?"

Nose to the ground, I tried to sniff the thing out.

"Don't look like the cat that swallowed the mouse...Ha!..Ha! That's mine, that milk. You didn't even ask per-r-r-mis-s-s-sion to have some."

Shivers rushed through me as I frantically circled in the darkness trying to find the owner of that scary voice.

There was a rustle of curtains, then a tall blue-gray cat strutted forward revealing herself and taking a deep bow. She spoke ever so slowly rolling her r's and s's in such a way that it reminded me of how slowly Granny Muriel let molasses ooze over her pancakes.

"I'm CAT-r-r-r-r-r-ina, the theatre cat. So nice of you to visit, but I r-r-r-r-eally must ask you to leave. The actors are all very kind, but two creatures around here are s-s-s-s-u-r-r-r-r-ly two, too many. So be on your way young pup and don't look back"

And with that she slinked over to the saucer of milk, butted me out of the way and sipped delicately proclaiming the remainder of the milk as her own until there wasn't a drop left. Satisfied, she licked each side of her mouth with her long, pointy tongue used much the same way humans wipe their mouths with napkins. Then she turned away from the bowl as if expecting pesky me to be gone.

I stood mesmerized by her poise and the rhythmic way she lapped at the bowl of milk. I've never seen a creature so sure of herself. She gazed with shiny green eyes in my direction, blinked her long luxurious eyelashes as if surprised that I hadn't heeded the warning and disappeared. Her liquid voice seemed to echo in the hall as she interrogated me.

"What! S-s-still here? Are you per-r-r-r--haps los-s-s-st? Do you want something? Attention maybe? Oh, yes-s-s-s-s that's it, attention. Well, in that ca-s-s-s-s-e, you have indeed come to the r-r-r-r-ight place. See those glittery people taking their places behind the curtain? That red curtain is about to open and they are going out on that stage where they will get lots of love and applause from a very large crowd."

LOVE did she say? My ears perked up.

"Oh, yes-s-s-s, did I whet your appetite? Poor little funny looking pup with your long body and stubby legs; you are looking for love and applause like the actors do. Fine, then all you have to do is join the glittery actors onstage and I p-r-r-r-r-o-m-i-s-s-s-s-s-e the audience will *l-o-v-e* you."

I backed away, not sure if this blue-gray CATrina cat was to be trusted.

She coaxed, "Go! Go out there. Take center stage r-r-right in front of the glittery people so that audience can see you first. I'm sure there will be one, maybe even some people who will consider your strange stature appealing enough to offer you the love you seek."

I looked toward the stage and that closed giant red curtain in front of the glittery people who were now in position and ready to perform for the waiting crowd.

"Why the hesitation? There's nothing to fear. Go forth and find your new family," CATrina coaxed.

My ears perked up. My new family! Oh, how could this CATrina cat guess what I wanted most of all was a family to love me. Could this theatre cat be right? Maybe she is being kind to me; maybe she is trying to help me. After all, she has no reason to want to hurt me.

"Look, that curtain is about to open. Decide!" CATrina insisted. "Are you going center s-s-s-stage to find your new loving family or are you going to cower in the dark corner miss-s-sing what might be your only chance?"

I looked again at that red curtain and the glittery people, then I looked back at CATrina who stared me down through furrowed brows and sneered lips obviously disappointed by my hesitation.

Suddenly music erupted. A swooshing sound filled the air as the curtains slowly glided open inviting enthusiastic applause from the audience.

"Now's your chance. Take it or leave it, it's all the same to me," she announced, and with that CATrina gave a shrug of her shoulder, turned on her haunches and indignantly started to saunter off.

Now's your chance!...Now's your chance!... Now's your chance! CATrina's words echoed in my ears.

I'm going to do it!

It's now!

Now or never!

A family to **LOVE** me!

Maybe they're out there!

YES, they're out there!

I'm sure they're out there now!

NOW!!!!!!

I rushed out, center stage, eager for that crowd to see me...anxious for my new family to realize I was the pup they were looking for. The bright lights blinded me. I could hardly see the audience for the lights.

But I heard it, a loud **GASP** from the crowd as if they collectively couldn't catch their breath.

"HHHHHHHHHHAAAAAAAAA!!!!"

The glittery people froze in their poses. I heard them whispering to each other, "How did that pup get in here? Someone grab that rascal! Get it out…Get it out…!"

I didn't know what to do. My feet felt stuck in the middle of that enormous stage.

And that's when I heard it. At first it was a whisper, but the whisper grew louder and louder. Now, I could hear the audience shouting.

"Look! Do you see what I see?"

"There's a pup in the middle of the stage. Look! Look!"

The glittery people from behind me continued whispering, "Where did that pup come from?"

"Someone get that dog!" The glittery people sounded menacing.

"Get that dog out of here!"

"Hurry! Hurry!"

I was confused.

The people in the audience didn't like me. They didn't clap for me. And the glittery people seemed mean.

I HAD TO GET OUT OF HERE! I HAD TO GET AWAY.....

RIGHT NOW!!

My feet became unstuck and I ran off the stage plowing headlong into CATrina. I had all I could do to keep from crying as I asked, "Why?!!"

She hissed, "S-S-S-S-K-A-T!"

CATrina cackled as I dodged the time man's outstretched hands that tried to grab me. I flew down the hall and I lunged down those stairs jumping two steps at a time. Over my shoulder, I could still hear gasps from the glittery people and the audience.

I didn't look back. I dashed to that S-T-A-G-E-D-O-O-R, but it was shut! How could I get out of here and away from all of those mean people? Racing footsteps grew louder as they thumped down the stairs. I hid behind the staircase. It was the time man again. He opened the stage door and that was my chance. I darted from behind the stairs and shot out the door! I *raaaaaan* and *raaaaaan* as fast as I could.

The time man shouted, "Hey, you, get back here! Get back here!"

But I wasn't about to do that. I kept running until my legs became wobbly. I stood panting, trying to catch my breath.

What just happened? Why was CATrina so mean to me? Why were the glittery people so nasty? Why didn't the audience like me either? I really try to be good so people will like me.

Why can't I find a family who wants me?

Am I really so ugly that no one will love me?

I don't understand.

I don't understand anything!

I MAKE FRIENDS AT THE CENTRAL PARK ZOO

SHRIEKING NOISES FROM more of those yellow cars startled me as I hiked down yet another busy street. I was lost and homesick. I missed Momma, Granny Muriel and the grandkids so much, but I couldn't go back to the farm even if I could find my way home.

I wanted someone to love me and take care of me the way that lady took care of the lucky curly pup. I hoped there might be a new family in that Broadway theatre, but they all turned out to be mean and scary.

What should I do?

Where could I go for *LOVE*?

Where could I find my new family?

I walked aimlessly on and on, whimpering with my every step.

OUCH!

My paws burned from scraping them on hot cement. Big tears flooded my eyes and I had to blink many times to see through them. I was so tired that my head kept flopping down, but I continued on.

Hot cement! Miles and miles of hot cement!

Wait a minute! My paws! They stopped burning! I looked up and shook my head once, then again.

GRASS!

GRASS EVERYWHERE!

I was standing on the edge of a very large grassy park spotted with tall trees. It reminded me of playing in Granny Muriel's yard.

WHAT LUCK!

I hugged the lawn, feeling coolness against my belly, then rolled onto my back wiggling against the tall blades of grass letting them scratch me. I stood upright again and looked around. What was this place?

There were other dogs, some were catching big round flying things that people threw to them. A boy called out to his dog, "Catch the Frisbee, Merlin!" And with that he threw a round disc to the dog who sprang into action and caught the object in his teeth. The boy burst into laughter and praised, "Good dog, Merlin!" It looked like so much fun. I wished someone would play with me like that.

I padded over a hill and was met with another surprise, just as wonderful as the first. At the foot of the hill was a big lake. My parched mouth drooled at the sight of so much water. I scooted down the hill, jumped into that lake and lapped at the water. Ah! It felt so good on my dry mouth and hot paws. I swam with arms outstretched letting my head bob in and out of the water. I swam in circles, then paddled way out, turned on my back and the water carried me toward shore.

As I started to swim out one more time, some rock-like thing bumped into me. What did I crash into? I jerked my head up and sniffed furiously at the air searching for clues. Then right in front of me it was as if the water parted and the strangest creature I had ever seen rose up from the depths. He had a round head, bulging eyes, a long out-stretched neck and his body was covered with a hard shell. He floated past me sluggishly rowing his oar-like arms. He blinked as if waking from a deep sleep and gazed in my direction. "Nice day for a swim," he drawled and a glimmer of a smile passed across his mouth.

"Ah, yes it is."

"This your first time here?"

"Yes, and it's the first time I've ever seen anyone like you."

That must have amused him, because he let out a big laugh and responded, "Oh, well then, let me introduce myself. I'm Slow Pete and I'm a turtle. This lake is my home. In fact, it's the home of my entire family. But you are very welcome to refresh yourself on this hot day."

"Thank you very much. I didn't know anyone lived here."

"You look like a young pup. I'm sure there are lots of things you don't know yet."

"That's for sure."

"In fact, you seem much too young to be on your own. I would invite you to join us, but you will get tired of swimming soon and I don't think you'll be happy living on a log. Well, it was nice meeting you, but I must be on my way. Enjoy your swim and take good care." And with that he dunked his head under the water and was gone.

I climbed out of the lake and shook my soaked coat. Then I looked back at the pond for Slow Pete, but he was gone. I started down a path that curved and passed through a dark tunnel. On the other side, there was a big sign with the letters **Z-O-O**.

Continuing beyond the **Z-O-O** sign was a pool with a man feeding really big fish. They jumped in and out of the water and made a loud "Augh! Augh! Augh!" sound as they clapped their fins together. Hunger returned and I wished that man would give me some of what he was feeding those fish. Starvation was far worse than being caught by that man, so I approached him.

The man glanced down in my direction and his eyes grew wide as he exclaimed, "Well, what have we here?! Where are your owners? Are you all alone?" I sniffed at the pail with the food in it, so he asked, "Hey, little pup, are you hungry? Do you want some of these?"

He tossed me some of what he had in his pail. It tasted salty, *hum...*fishy. But it sure was better than nothing. Then the man put a bowl of water down and I drank it all up. That fishy taste made me real thirsty.

The man patted my forehead as he asked, "You're such a pretty dachshund, but what are you doing all alone in this big city?"

I stared up at him. He had kind eyes, so I let him pet me. Then he started to pet the back of my neck and that's when he noticed, "Well, what have we here? Are you part dachshund and part

Rhodesian Ridgeback? I've never seen a dachs-hund with a ridge on the back of its neck?"

I backed away from him. With all that happened to me, I had forgotten about that scruff.

"Oh, no, don't shy away," the man implored.

Then he called out, "Hey, George, look at who's here."

Another man came over and looked down at me. "Cute pup," he remarked. "Where'd she come from?"

"She just turned up and she was so hungry and thirsty," the first man answered.

"Well, do you want a dog, Larry?"

"Oh, no, we can't just keep her. She might belong to someone."

"Well, how do we find out?" George asked.

Larry thought for a minute then came up with a plan. "My wife works at the Fifth Avenue Pet Store. We need to see if this little pup's got a locator chip in her. I imagine someone is very upset about losing a pup like this one even with her ridge."

"Good idea."

"After work I'll take the pup to Audrey's store."

Then Larry knelt down, pet me and said, "Don't worry, little one. We'll find your true home, if you have one."

I licked his cheek. Larry was kinder to me than anyone had been since I left Granny Muriel's farm. He picked me up, carried me inside a building and to a big kitchen. There he opened a refrigerator door, took out a brown bag and offered, "I just happen to have a nice meatball sandwich in here. I'd be happy to split it with you if you want." Larry opened the sandwich and took out two meatballs, cut them up and put them on a plate for me. I sniffed at them and gave them a few licks. They tasted so good that I gobbled them right up.

He laughed and commented, "I sort of figured you'd be hungry, but I didn't know you were starving." He looked at the remainder of the sandwich, and then back at me. After a moment of thought, he continued, "I guess you're hungrier than I am, so you can have what's left."

He cut up the rest and put them in the bowl for me. Boy, they were the best meatballs I'd ever eaten! When I finished, Larry pet me some more then said, "Come on. I have to work for a bit longer, then we'll go visit Audrey at the pet store."

I had fun following Larry. He took me to one building that had a forest inside with lots of brightly colored birds flying around.

"This place is called the Rain Forest Pavilion," Larry told me.

He pointed out some of the birds and called them by name, "Fairy Blue Birds and Scarlet-chested Parrots."

He took me to another section and explained, "Here's where we keep the monkeys. We have Colobus Monkeys and Tamarins. Just look at how human-like they are."

Then Larry added, "Well, it's time to feed the animals at the children's zoo."

So off we went to another part of the zoo. We went through tall iron gates that led to a corral filled with fuzzy animals.

Larry said, "And here we have the sheep. There's a new member of the sheep family I want you to meet." He took me to a corner of the corral where there was a lamb drinking from a pail.

Larry introduced us by saying, "This here's Candy. She was born about three months ago, so she's a little one just like you.

Now, stay right here while I feed the sheep."
Larry went to the back of the corral to get
the food.

"Hi," Candy greeted me in a friendly
high-pitched voice.

"How do you do?"

"Are you going to live here with us?"

"I don't know. But I'd like to."

"I like it here, but then again, I haven't
lived anywhere else. Where did you come
from?"

"A place real far away."

"Maybe you can stay here. Then we could
play all day. Did you meet Mo yet?"

"No, who's Mo?"

"Mo is what's called a Llama. Come on,
I'll introduce you."

Candy took me to another part of the corral where there was a very tall, very wooly looking animal who craned his neck over the fence to get a carrot that a little boy was offering him. Candy got Mo's attention so he chewed the carrot up fast and ambled over to us.

"Mo, I want you to meet my new friend."

"Hi," Mo greeted me in a very deep voice.

"And this is...oh...that's right. I didn't catch your name."

I thought for a minute and it was the first time I realized I didn't think I had a name. "I'm sorry, but I don't know what my name is."

"That's all right," Mo assured me. "It's nice to meet you anyway. What are you?"

That was another confusing question, but I thought hard then answered, "Well, Larry called me a dachshund and, in fact,

Granny Muriel called me a dachshund too. So, I guess that's what I am."

"Hmm, a dachshund?" Mo thought for a moment then admitted, "I've never heard of that animal. I think you're the first of its kind here. Are you going to stay?"

"I wish I could. Everyone has been so nice to me since I came to this park and the zoo."

"Maybe you can stay," Candy suggested. "It's fun here. We get treats from all the kids who come to visit with their parents. They're all so nice to us, you'll see."

"I could use another carrot right now, so if you'll excuse me," said Mo as he strolled off to the edge of the corral where there was a gathering of children who held out carrots and apple pieces for him to munch on.

I wish I could stay here with Larry and my new friends, Candy and Mo. For the first time in a long time, I was really having fun.

But Larry soon returned, looked at his watch and declared, "Well, my little doxie friend, I hate to cut your visit short, but we should go see Audrey. Hopefully we can help you find your way back home."

AUDREY'S PET STORE

LARRY CARRIED ME down a path that led to a busy street. He held me tight so I wouldn't fall from his arms. I felt safe with Larry, so I rested my head on his shoulder and sniffed at his hair. His smell was strong from a combination of all the animals Larry cared for at the zoo and it made me feel secure and happy. More of those yellow cars honked and whizzed by, but I wasn't afraid this time now that I had Larry to protect me. He carried me inside a store that was lined with pups in cages. It was sad seeing them all locked up the way I had been in that carry case. Did they ever get out to play?

He brought me to a lady behind the counter. "Hi, Hon, here's my little orphan,." He announced as he handed me over to her.

"Such a lovely little girl at that," Audrey replied as she stroked my head. "Surely someone is looking for you. Now then, let's see what we can find out." She held a wand looking thing up to my neck as if expecting to hear something. She shook her head "no" and reported, "I can't seem to find it. Too bad, but this little one doesn't have a locator chip." And with that she handed me back to Larry.

Larry brushed my ears back and sounded sad as he asked, "What are we going to do?"

"We'll put a sign up here at the store and signs around town. We could place an ad in the local paper and contact the pound to see if someone looked for her there. She's such a sweet pup, she must belong to someone."

Larry held me up so he could look directly into my eyes and confided, "I'm sure someone is looking for you, but just between you and me, I wish I could keep you. You're such a spunky little girl to make it around this big city all alone."

Then Larry looked from me to his wife and asked, "Why can't we do that? Why can't we be her new family?"

Audrey shook her head "no" and answered, "Oh, Honey, I certainly would say 'sure' if we didn't have two dogs already. Remember the trouble the condo board gave us when we adopted the second? They'll throw us out if we try to bring a third into our tiny apartment. But maybe we can help her get the loving family she deserves. No locator chip means no history. I can't sell a dog here at the shop without registration papers. But Matt Flynn from the animal shelter out on Long Island is coming to town. We could send this little one off with him. He'll hold her while we search for her owners. Then if no one comes forward, she'll be placed for adoption.

Larry sighed, held me up to face him and consoled me with, "I'm sorry we can't keep you, but on Long Island you'll find a family with a big backyard instead of a tiny New York apartment. You'll be happy then." He kissed my forehead and I licked at his cheek. I wanted to stay with Larry. But he handed me over to Audrey who put me in a cage with some other pups. They circled and smelled the city streets on me. I felt sad again being locked up in this cage.

I curled up in a corner and fell asleep until I woke from the sound of the cage door opening. Audrey picked me up, gave a hug then transferred me to a carry case. She handed it to a man and said, "Take good care of our girl, Matt."

Oh, No!

Here I am again in another one of those dark, scary carry cases!

I'M ON THE ROAD AGAIN

I COULDN'T SEE who carried me. All I could
see was the busy road with whizzing traffic. I
was taken to a long white van and put in the
back next to a few more cages with pups who
must also be going to that Long Island place.
We were off and I looked out the window at
lots of those yellow cars speeding by. Then
we went into a tunnel and when we came
out, I didn't see any more yellow cars. I was
stuck in that cage and getting pretty restless.
I tried looking at the cages next to me, but
I couldn't see the other pups. I could hear
them moving around though and some were
whimpering. I sniffed at the corners of my

cage and got the scent of dogs on either side of me.

Was this cage as easy to open as the one on the airplane? I spread my paw out real wide like before and hit the lock.

OUCH! That hurt!

I'm not trying that again. Anyway, where would I go? I was so far away from home and I didn't even know how to find Larry and Audrey now. But they were nice and I don't think they would send me to a bad place. Maybe Larry was right and I'm going to where I'll get a loving family all my own.

Nothing left for me to do but wait and see.

ME AND THE LONG ISLAND ANIMAL SHELTER

WE MADE A TURN, got off the long road and took a few more turns. There were trees all around and houses with grass in front of them. One thing was for sure, we weren't in that city anymore. The van slowed down, then came to a halt. The driver got out and headed towards a green door. I paced back and forth, trying to get a better look at where we were.

Low buildings with white fronts and green shutters lined the street. In one of the windows, I saw something moving. Pups! They were hopping over each other and playing just the way I used to play with my brothers and sisters. That made me homesick. How I wished I could go back to Granny Muriel's farm with Momma and all of my brothers and sisters. If I could have that again, I wouldn't even mind if they got fed before me. I really wouldn't! But my old home could never be the same. My brothers and sisters were gone. Granny Muriel didn't want me or she wouldn't have sent me away.

I hope Momma is OK and I hope she doesn't miss me too much.

If only I could find a new family all my own and kids to play with like Tommy and Katie and a Mommy and Daddy to hug me.

The driver returned and opened up the back of the van. He took the cages out, one at a time, and carried them into the building. Soon, he came to me. I was carried inside where there were lots of pups in cages lined up behind a counter. It looked very much like Audrey's store except that there weren't just pups here. I could see big dogs, too, in crates on the floor. The driver put my cage on the counter and opened the door as he talked to a lady and the girl standing next to her.

"Oh, Stella, Cheryl, look at this one here. This doxie came from Audrey's pet store. Actually she's a stray; Larry just turned around and there she was at the zoo. If no one claims her in a week's time, we can put her up for adoption."

"Poor little thing. I wonder if there's a very sad family missing this pup?" The voice of the woman, Stella, sounded concerned.

"She's so tiny. Anything could have happened to her while she was loose in that big city," Cheryl insisted.

"Yeah, but she's safe now," said Stella as she took me out of my cage. "And if no family comes forward within the week, we'll find a nice home for this little one."

Just then, Cheryl touched the back of my neck and remarked, "What's that?"

"Looks like she's got a little scruff."

"Will that scruff disappear in time?"

"No, it will probably just get bigger as she grows up."

"Well, she's quite pretty anyway, even with that scruff. I wish I could take her home, but Mom would kill me if I brought home another dog."

Stella chuckled as she replied, "We can't keep them all, but we can help them find forever homes. That's what we need to do for this little girl, too, if her owners don't show up. Why don't you put her in the cage with the brown terrier and the tan Chihuahua pups. That way she'll have some playmates her own size."

And with that, I was handed over to Cheryl who brought me to one of the cages behind the counter. "Here you go now," Cheryl cheerily uttered as she opened the cage door. "Have fun with your new buddies and I promise to come back to play with you a little later."

I can't believe I traveled all this way just to be stuck in another cage!

As soon as Cheryl locked the cage door, the other two pups came right over and sniffed at me. I stood quite still letting them take a whiff, then introduced myself by sniffing back. Soon we were in a smelling match, but their noses tickled making me giggle.

"You're tickling me!" I laughed and shook myself.

"You smell funny," the brown pup discovered as he sniffed at me.

"Where did you come from?" the tan pup asked.

"I don't know, but there were lots of tall buildings. I didn't like it too much until I went to this zoo thing. A nice man took me in, but he couldn't keep me, so they sent me here."

"It's not so bad here. They give us plenty of food and a warm place to stay," the brown pup assured.

"Yeah, and we play a lot," the tan pup added.

And without any warning, he jumped at me. I jumped back. The brown pup put a paw out and touched my back. I put my paw on the brown pup's outstretched paw, then we chased and climbed over each other. I was part of a pack again and I loved it. Though these two weren't my brothers or sisters, I loved playing with my new friends all the same. In fact, except for my time with Larry and the zoo, I hadn't been this happy since I was at Granny Muriel's farm. I guess this cage wasn't as bad as I thought it was going to be.

Cheryl did come back like she promised. She took me out, petted me and commented, "You're such a pretty little thing. I can't believe you were loose in New York City! I would be afraid if I were alone in a big place like that. But I'm glad you're here with us now. If you don't have someone looking for you, I'm sure a nice family will see how sweet you are and you won't be here for too long."

And with that, Cheryl brought me back to my new buddies. We did our sniffing routine again, then went back to playing and chasing each other as much as we could in the space we had. Soon, we got tired and curled up with backs touching. I gave a great big sigh. I was comfortable with my new friends. This was the first time in so long that I got to sleep feeling the warmth and softness of surrounding pups.

I was happy.

I woke up to voices as Stella and Cheryl opened the front door in the morning. They said something about Audrey calling and having "no luck" finding my family. I could have told them that a week ago. It seems that now I'm up for adoption if someone wants me. But I wasn't too sure about that, after all, in the past week, people looked at me, but no one seemed interested enough to want to take me home. At first I thought it must have something to do with that scruff, but my crate mates were still here, too, and they looked perfect to me. Maybe that wasn't it, but if not that, then what?

My pals and I were in a regular routine now. Stella and Cheryl came in each morning, turned on the lights and made their rounds giving us fresh water bottles and food. With only two other pups, I didn't have to back off much to let the others eat. In fact, they made room for me and we all ate together. It was better than waiting for the others to get theirs first.

Just like every other day for the past week now, people came into the shelter. Some would stop in front of our cage and comment. People said, "See the pretty pups. They're all so cute, aren't they?"

A little boy stretched his neck trying to get a closer look at us. He sounded excited as he called to his mother, "Mom, come over here! Look at the dachshund. I want to hold it."

"You sure you want to see a dachshund? They do have a beagle," the mother replied.

And his brother rushed over asking, "How about a Lab? Come on, they have one in the next room. The lady said it's about a year old and house broken."

"Oh, Mom, let's see the dachshund first," the boy implored.

Stella came over and asked the mother, "Do you want to see her?"

"Well, yes, I guess so. We can look at the dachshund first."

Stella reached into our cage and took me out. She handed me to the little boy and told the mother that she could take me to one of the rooms set up for playing with pups. The boy sat on the floor with me on his lap. He patted my forehead softly. I liked him.

"You're such a nice pup," he murmured in my ear, "Isn't she a nice pup, Mom?"

The mother patted my back, but was hesitant. "Yes, she is. But I don't think we should just take the first pup we see. Let's consider her, but look around a bit more first. Your brother is still out there with the Lab and I would like to see what other dogs they have here. We really won't be able to make the final decision anyway until we come back with Dad when he gets out of work."

"OK, let's look some more. But my vote is for this little red dachshund," the boy insisted.

"We'll see, we'll see. We're all going to have to decide together as a family."

"OK. OK." The boy sounded disappointed.

With that, he handed me back to his mom. I licked her cheek thinking she might like me better if I did that. But all she said was, "How sweet."

She brought me back to Stella who asked, "So, what do you think? She's a sweet little girl, isn't she?"

"That she is," the mother answered, "But I've never seen a dachshund with a scruff. Anyway, we haven't made up our minds yet. We'll have to see."

As the mother handed me back to Stella, I caught sight of a family looking at the cages behind the counter. There was a mom, a dad, a little boy and a little girl. The boy and girl reminded me of Tommy and Katie.

My eyes met the eyes of the little girl's. A strange feeling came over me. It was as if she was talking to me with her eyes. They were warm and gentle and I could almost hear her say something to me though her lips didn't move. She just looked at me. I looked back from behind the cage door and I could see her smile. But maybe it was all in my head, because the family didn't ask to see me. And a moment later, they were gone.

Wow! That was strange! I didn't know that little girl. I've never seen her before, but all the same, there was something familiar about her.

Other people came and went. A few asked to see me. One more person remarked about my scruff.

Won't they ever forget about that?!

Madison Weatherbee- The Different Dachshund

MY PREMONITION

THAT NIGHT AFTER Stella turned off the lights and locked the shelter door, I curled up with my back against one of my buddies and fell into a deep sleep.

In my dream, I was outside running in soft grass, chasing a ball. I scooped it up into my mouth, turned and ran to the person playing with me. And there he was-the little boy I had seen with his sister in the shelter. I dropped the ball at his feet and ran back waiting for him to throw it to me. He chuckled, picked up the ball and tossed it. I jumped up and caught it in my mouth making him laugh and applaud my stunt.

That's when I heard it, a voice calling out and it was calling out to me although I had never heard the name before.

"**Madison**, come here. Beautiful, **Madison Weatherbee**, it's time for your brushing."

I didn't know who **Madison Weatherbee** was, but I looked in the direction of the voice. Standing on a deck by the back door of the house was the little girl I had seen in the shelter. I ran to her, like I knew her. She took my face in her hands and covered me with kisses as she murmured, "My beauty girl, let me brush you."

We sat on the top step of the deck and she bent over me with a brush. The soft brushing felt so good on my back. The little boy joined us. He sat there waiting for my grooming to be over so we could get back to our game.

She delighted in telling her brother, "Just look how shiny she is when I brush her. I love brushing her magnificent mane."

87

She touched my scruff with her hand and added, "Her mane is so soft."

Her brother chimed in saying, "There are no other dachshunds in the entire world with a magnificent mane like hers. She's the most special dachshund I've ever seen."

They called my scruff a magnificent mane and they seemed to like it. They treated it as if it was something wonderful and not something ugly. I stretched and sighed in contentment. I liked this boy and girl. I liked them a lot.

Sliding glass doors opened and the sweet, inviting voice of their mother called out, "Come on, you three. It's time for dinner. Daddy should be home any minute."

As we scooted inside, the mom picked me up, hugged me and beamed, "Oh, you're such a good, smart girl. You come the first time I call, my beautiful *Madison*…"

Creaking noises and the clicking on of lights disturbed my dream. It was Stella opening up for another day. Oh, why did Stella have to wake me? Why couldn't I stay in that happy dream **...FOREVER...?**

BACK TO REALITY

I BLINKED MY EYES. I was still in this shelter, still in the cage.

But that dream felt so real.

feel like
dream is real

The little boy and little girl were real. I __know__ that. I'd seen them here with their mom and dad. I want to be as happy as I was in that dream. I wish they would come back for me and take me home with them. I wish I could play ball with the little boy and have that little girl brush my scruff and call it a magnificent mane. I would love the mom to hug me and tell me how good I am. I wish I could have a forever family like that one.

But it was nothing more than a very real-feeling dream. Just a dream...that's all it was...just a dream.

Forget it!

Forget playing ball with that little boy and getting brushed by that little girl. I'm not going to get the mom's hugs and yummy dinner.

And who is **Madison Weatherbee** anyway?

Cheryl opened the cage and placed our breakfast down. I shouldn't complain, at least I had someone to feed me. But I couldn't help wondering what that mom in my dream was giving **Madison Weatherbee** for dinner. I'd bet it was something mighty good. Stella turned the white rectangular sign from *CLOSED* to *OPEN* and people shuffled in to look at us.

My two pals and I decided to have a monkey-in-the-middle game The idea was to put one of us in the middle then scramble around to see who got pinned first. The winner would get to eat the rest of our breakfast without the other two sneaking around for a bite. When I was in the middle, I ran so fast that neither of them could catch me. Then the tan pup put out a foot to trip me, but I was too fast. I jumped over her foot and landed on top of the food bowl sending kibble flying in all directions. We settled for a moment. The prize was gone now! I went to the water bowl and had a good, long drink. All this playing made me so thirsty. As I drank, I heard voices that sounded familiar.

Then I heard Stella's voice ask, "Can I show you a pup?"

I stopped drinking and looked out from behind the bars of the cage. To my surprise there was that little girl, that little boy and the mom and dad who were in the store yesterday and in my dreams last night!

I couldn't let them go again without seeing me. I had to do something, but what could I do stuck here in this cage. Then the idea came to me. I could sit way up on my hind legs. Sit up *s-s-s-s-o-o-o-o* tall that they couldn't miss me when they looked in this direction.

"What are you doing?" the brown pup asked.

"I want them to see me."

"Why do you care?" pried the tan pup.

"I just do."

I heard the mom say, "We were here yesterday looking at all the dogs."

The little girl laughed and called out, "Look! Look at that pup!" She pointed in my direction. Yes, she saw me, I got her attention. I stood on my hind legs and stretched so much that I filled up the cage.

I stood way up.

I stood up **TALL**.

I stood up for a *lo-o-o-o-o-n-g, lo-o-o-o-o-n-g* time.

"Wow!" the boy exclaimed. "How long can that pup stand up like that?"

"She's so cute! Can we see her?" the little girl asked.

"Yes! Can we see that one?" the little boy agreed.

"She's amazing. I've never seen a pup stand up on hind legs that long," the dad remarked.

"Well, I think you got your wish. They see you," observed the tan pup.

I stretched as far up as my long body would go.

"Would you like to see that dachshund?" Stella asked.

"Yes! Oh, yes! Could we?" the little boy and little girl pleaded.

The parents smiled and the dad answered, "I think that one is a hit with my family already."

As Stella handed me over to the dad, the little girl blurted out, "She's the one from yesterday! Oh, I was hoping she would still be here."

The dad laughed and commented, "Hmm. It seems as if our Kimmy had this all planned out."

The dad held me while Kimmy, her brother and the mom petted me.

"Why don't you all get acquainted in the petting room over there," Stella suggested.

"Would you like to do that?" the dad asked.

"Yes! Oh, yes!" both kids chimed in.

MADISON WEATHERBEE GETS A HOME

IN THE PETTING room, they all sat down on the floor with me in the middle. Kimmy kissed my forehead and her brother petted my neck. The mom held my face in her hands and said, "Look how beautiful she is."

"Yes, she's a stunner all right," the dad agreed.

"She seems like such a perfect little angel," the mom put in.

"Well, she's even better than perfect. See that mane going down her neck?"

"Yes, it's quite obvious, but I think it makes her extra special. After all, I've never seen another dachshund with a mane like that."

Then the dad said, "Actually I have. When I was a boy, just about your age, Richie, I had a dachshund, our Penny. She was my very best friend, a great old girl with a very gentle way about her. But there was something extra special about Penny-she had a ridge going down the back of her neck, just like this little one. My father used to try to comb it flat. One day while we walked Penny in the local park, Dad stopped at a bench. He sat with Penny on his lap and once again tried to smooth out her ridge. A stranger passed by, saw what Dad was doing and told him that Penny's ridge was not something to hide. It was something to be proud of. It turned out that this lady was a dachshund breeder. She said the ridge is called a Hunter's Crest and it's a sign of 'good luck'! She said Penny should be allowed to wear her Hunter's Crest proudly. So you see, not only does this little girl have a Hunter's Crest just like Penny's, but it's a symbol of good luck."

"WOW! A Hunter's Crest!" Richie said in awe.

"I just love that she's different. I think she's perfect," Kimmy asserted.

"**Absolutely perfect**!" the dad agreed.

"And she knows tricks already! I've never seen a dog stand up for so long. I bet she can even play ball with me," Richie exclaimed.

I trotted over to Richie and gave him my paw.

"Look! She gives her paw!" the little boy shouted. "She's so smart."

"And I'll bet she's a good girl, too." the mom added as she picked me up and hugged me.

I couldn't believe I was really here with this family and it wasn't just a dream this time. I liked them, I liked them a lot and I didn't want them to go away leaving me behind. So while the mom hugged me, I put my paws around her neck, licked her cheek and rested my head on her shoulder.

"Just look, she's such a cuddly puppy," the mom crooned.

"And I think she's the perfect girl to see you two through your childhood, just like Penny was the perfect girl to see me through mine," the dad concluded.

"What do you want to call her?" asked the mom.

Kimmy held me up so she could look right into my eyes and she declared, "She looks like a **Madison** to me if I ever saw one."

Richie thought about it, then agreed, "**Madison**...yes, I think she is a **Madison**. I'll go along with that."

"Yes, her name is **Madison...MADISON WEATHERBEE**. She has our last name." Kimmy proclaimed.

"How perfect! **Madison Weatherbee!**" the mom declared.

"It's a good old family name. Come on, let's tell Stella?" the dad said with decision.

"Yes," the mom agreed, then turned to me and said, "We hope you'll like your new family, **Madison Weatherbee**."

"We'll do everything we can to make you very happy," Kimmy added.

I sat way up on my back legs again wanting to amuse my new family.

"There she goes again! She's amazing!" Richie called out.

And the rest of the family chuckled at my antics.

Stella opened the petting room door to see the family entertained by me as I continued to sit way upright in the center of them.

"It sounded like our little one was putting on a show for you," she mused.

"Look what she can do!" Richie said as he pointed excitedly at me.

"She's a talented little girl at that," Stella commented.

"She's the **most perfect** dachshund we've ever seen!" Kimmy declared.

"So, what do you want to do?" Stella asked.

"We would love to adopt this beautiful little pup," the dad answered without hesitation.

"Congratulations!" Stella chirped. "You picked a very sweet doxie."

"And she's very lucky, too," Richie added.

"Well, I guess she is. She found herself a very nice family indeed," Stella replied.

"No, it's not that. See her ridge, Daddy says it's called a Hunter's Crest and it means good luck!" Richie blurted out.

"Well, what about that!" remarked Stella. "I didn't know there was a name for her scruff or that it meant something really good. Funny how many people passed her by because of it. But your family saw her difference as something good, something special."

"I think we *all* lucked out today," the mom concluded.

"Why don't I get her groomed while you fill out the application," Stella suggested.

Kimmy and the mom kissed my forehead, the dad and Richie petted me. Then I was passed to Stella who brought me to the back room where they shampooed me and put a big pink bow around my neck. Stella returned and marveled, "My, don't you look beautiful and, my little lucky one, you are getting a dear family who loves you very much already." And with that she scooped me up and carried me back to my new family who had loaded themselves up with food bowls, a red leash and harness, lots of stuffed toys all for me and a beautiful red

coat, just as beautiful as the one the curly pup had on! Stella gave me over to the mom amongst lots of *o-o-o-h-s* and *a-a-a-h-s* from Kimmy and Richie.

The mom hugged me and cooed, "Oh, look! Just look at how beautiful she is, all groomed and soft! And such a pretty pink bow."

Kimmy and Richie petted me and the dad said, "I brought my camera along for just in case. Everyone, look this way. I want to take Madison's coming home picture with the entire family."

Stella interrupted, "But it isn't truly a family picture without you in it." Then offered, "Why don't I take the picture?"

So there we were in our first family photograph together with me in my new pink bow being cuddled by Kimmy, while Richie petted me and my new mom and dad stood on either side of us.

AND as Stella snapped away, I couldn't help thinking maybe this Hunter's Crest did bring good luck. After all, what a lucky pup I was to be the newest member of the
Weatherbee family

...........................**FOREVER!**

THE END

MADISON'S MESSAGE T

Don't let your difference get you down.
Embrace it like a sunny day.
It is a gift to keep around.
To help you learn in many ways.
You soon will thank your lucky stars,
That you are not like all the rest.
Be proud and share with near and far
What you learned from your tough test.
If you are good to all you meet
The world will open up for you
And usher in new friends to greet
They'll bring insights you never knew.
My message is for all to see.
Be kind, be thoughtful, it's so easy.

BARBARA ANNE KIRSHNER
AUTHOR AND PHOTOGRAPHER

Barbara Anne Kirshner is an educator who has enjoyed teaching all grade levels from elementary through college. Barbara is passionately dedicated to animal advocacy and volunteers for rescue groups on Long Island. She is thrilled every time she helps a wonderful animal find its forever home. Barbara lives in Miller Place, New York with her husband, Gregg, and their three adorable dachshunds, Lexington, Park, and Melissa Tulip, who expect to see their stories in print real soon.

KIMBERLY ANN MCKENNA
ILLUSTRATOR

Kimberly Ann McKenna is a graphic designer and graduate of Farmingdale College. Special thanks go to Kim for her creative interpretation and heart-warming illustrations in *Madison Weatherbee*. Kim lives in Bethpage with her husband, Mike, and their beloved cat, Cilo.

Made in the USA
Middletown, DE
17 December 2016